I Look for Mark

Written by Susan Frame
Illustrated by Valeria Issa

Collins

I look for Mark in his room.

Mark

2

I dash into the garden.

4

I look near the rocket.

I can not see Mark.

Jibber barks.

He barks at the chair.

Look! A coat with feet and hair!

Is it Mark?

Yes! Mark is in the coat.

Meet Mark.

Look for Mark

After reading

Letters and Sounds: Phase 3
Word count: 54
Focus phonemes: /ee/ /oa/ /oo/ /oo/ /ar/ /or/ /ow/ /ear/ /air/ /er/
Common exception words: I, no, into, the, he, and
Curriculum links: Understanding the world; Personal, social and emotional development
Early learning goals: Reading: read and understand simple sentences; use phonic knowledge to decode regular words and read them aloud accurately; read some common irregular words

Developing fluency

- Your child may enjoy hearing you read the book. Use a child's voice for the story, a surprised tone for the exclamations on page 10, and a questioning voice for page 11.
- Ask your child to reread their favourite pages aloud. Encourage them to read expressively, and to look out for exclamation marks and question marks as clues for how to read those sentences.

Phonic practice

- Take turns to find and point to a word in which two letters make one sound, e.g. l/oo/k, r/oo/m, g/ar/d/e/n, s/ee, c/oa/t. The other sounds out and reads the word.
- Challenge your child to find and read the two words in which three letters stand for one sound. (page 6: n/ear, page 9: ch/air, page 10: h/air)

Extending vocabulary

- Ask your child to say the opposite (antonym) for each word:
  - page 4 – **dash** (*creep, walk slowly, saunter*)
  - page 4 – **into** (*out of, away from*)
  - page 6 – **near** (*far from, away from*)
  - page 9 – **he** (*she*)